# This igloo book belongs to:

....................................

# igloobooks

*Published in 2013*
*by Igloo Books Ltd*
*Cottage Farm*
*Sywell*
*NN6 0BJ*
*www.igloobooks.com*

*Copyright © 2013 Igloo Books Ltd*

*FIR003 0713*
*2 4 6 8 10 9 7 5 3*
*ISBN 978-1-78197-470-4*

*Illustrated by Sarah Pitt and Monika Filipina*
*Written by Carrie Lewis*

*Printed and manufactured in China*

# Big Nelly

igloobooks

Nelly the elephant loved to play with her three best friends,
Stripes the tiger, Jo-Jo the monkey and Kiki the parrot, but
whenever she did, things seemed to go wrong.

The friends had so much fun together, but Nelly felt much too big to join in. Her size had become a very BIG problem.

When they played hide-and-seek, Jo-Jo the monkey hid up a tree and Kiki the parrot pretended to be a pretty flower, but Nelly couldn't hide anywhere at all.

Her big ears flapped out
from either side of the
tree trunk...

... her bottom poked out from behind
the bushes...

... and her nose
stuck out like a
snake in the grass.

Poor Nelly couldn't find
anywhere to hide!

At the swimming pool, Nelly cried, "HOORAY!" and ran towards the water in excitement. "I'll go first," she said, jumping in with a huge SPLASH!

The water went everywhere, leaving the pool empty.
"Oh, NELLY!" cried the others. "Now we can't swim!"
"I'm sorry," said Nelly, feeling a bit silly. "Let's play another game."

"I know," said Stripes. "Let's play tug-of-war." Kiki and Stripes picked up one end of the rope and Nelly and Jo-Jo picked up the other. "Ready, steady, PULL!" cried Stripes.

Nelly's friends HEAVED with all their strength. Then, Nelly gave one tiny tug and Kiki, Stripes and Jo-Jo were pulled over into a big pile. CRASH! "Oh dear," said Nelly.

"Let's try the swing instead," said Jo-Jo. "Come on, Nelly. We'll give you a push!" Jo-Jo, Kiki and Stripes pushed Nelly as hard as they could.

For a few seconds, Nelly hung happily in the air, then, suddenly, WHOOSH! The swing fell back down and knocked the three friends over with a WHOOMPH!

"WAAAH!" cried Nelly, bursting into tears. "It's no use! I'm too big to play with you. I'll just have to go and play by myself."

"Don't go!" her friends cried together, but it was too late.
Nelly was gone. She set off into the jungle, all alone.

Nelly plodded along all afternoon, singing songs to herself and catching butterflies with her trunk. After a little while, she began to feel lonely.

"I miss my friends," thought Nelly with a sigh.
"Being alone isn't half as fun as playing with Jo-Jo, Kiki and
Stripes, even if I am too big!"

Suddenly, Nelly heard a squawk. It was Kiki, flying straight towards her. "Kiki, what are you doing here?" cried Nelly, happily.

"It's an emergency," said Kiki. "Jo-Jo is stranded in the middle of the lake. Please come quickly. You're the only one big enough to help!"

Nelly raced through the trees and Kiki flapped her wings.
They rushed as fast as they could, until they reached the lake.

"Don't worry, Jo-Jo!" cried Nelly, jumping into the water. She waded to the rock that Jo-Jo was holding on to, wrapped her long trunk around him and carried him to the shore.

"Thank you, Nelly," said Jo-Jo. "You're the only one who could have saved me!" "Please don't go away again," said Kiki and Stripes, hugging Nelly tightly. "We missed you!"

Nelly smiled, feeling special. "I missed you too, but I'm still too big to play our games," she said. "It isn't the size of the friends, but the size of the friendship that counts," replied Jo-Jo.

From that day on, the friends only played
games that they could all join in with.
"Wahoo!" cried Nelly. "This is the best fun ever!"